The Wonderful Adventures of

Dondo the Magnificent

First story

"Dondo's New Friend"

There was a dog called Dondo, it didn't know if it was a boy or a girl or even a dog or a cat , have you ever thought if they do actually know if they are boys or girls, or dogs or maybe a cat? They don't know, they just are!

Dogs are only interested in two things, can you guess what they are?

So Dondo was a mixed breed, a real mixed up dog, with short hair, long snout with a waggley tail and a wet nose, big doleful eyes a brown and white coat and a wonky ear, but Dondo didn't care or really need to know.

Dondo's owner was a retired Lady, she loved her dog and to her it wouldn't matter if Dondo was a boy or a girl or a cat, well maybe not a cat, and he was of course to her just, Dondo the Magnificent!

Dondo was really loved, and very much so.

Dondo was a trusted companion for the owner, sleeping at her feet, keeping her warm at the bottom of the bed and playful enough to be a fun pet in the house and garden, and what a lovely home, it was situated at the end of a leafy lane called "leafy lane" and had a thatched roof comfortable beds and a long leafy cottage garden.

Dondo was as much at home on the foot of the bed overlooking the window ledge on a rainy day as he was in the garden on a sunny day sleeping under the apple tree.

Quite often Dondo would wake from a snoozey sleep in the

garden have a big yawn then to wobbly walk slowly up to the house take a drink of water out of the cool tin bowl, sniff the air with a twitchy nose, then sit, and wait. You could almost set your watch by this crafty move, every afternoon.

Nearly every day Dondo's owner would be cooking biscuits for the next day, then she would put a meat pie into the hot oven just to warm through for her dinner later that afternoon.

It within a few minutes would fill the house with a wonderful homely smell that would make any dog or human hungry.

This is the time Dondo would be extra loving, schmoozing up to the Lady, perhaps if the Schmoozing was good Dondo would get a warm squidgy biscuit. The schmoozing of course was always very good and for the most, always worked.

Dondo spent a lot of time sleeping, dreaming with twitching legs and little gruffs, chasing dreamy rabbits and scaring away imaginary pigeons from the long green garden.

Dondo was a kind hearted dog although dreams of chasing away animals from the garden was nice to dream, Dondo would never hurt any of them, just maybe to make friends. Dondo often thought that the dreams were a sleepy form of exercising, and quiet enjoyed them.

One day, Dondo was sleeping in a favourite hollow near the apple tree, the leaves on the tree made for a dappled gentle light from the warm breeze and the warm grass beneath Dondo was really cosy and made for the best sleepy nest for a rest.

All of a sudden Dondo's wonky ear sat straight up!

Boing!

As Dondo started to awake from the rabbit chase in a dream, Dondo heard a sound, at first Dondo couldn't work out if the noise was in the dream or was for real.

Then it made a sound again, Aaaawoooooo!

Aaaaawooooo!

It wasn't a growl or wasn't a howl, Dondo didn't know what it was.

Taking a look up towards the house, everything looked and sounded as normal,

Dondo listened again, Aaaawoooooo!

There it was again!

Such a strange noise, familiar but still not a sound Dondo could recognise or remember hearing this noise before.

Dondo's ears were now like radar twitching in all directions trying to locate the sound and where it might be coming from, was it to the left or to the right, was it straight ahead or coming from behind.

Dondo let out a short bark "rrrraagght!"

Within a few seconds the sound came again Aaaawoooooo and this time followed by "Aaaawoooooo rrrraagght"!

Dondo replied with a deeper "rrrraagght! Rrrraaougght"! woof!

Which in Dondo's mind he meant it this time, a sort of don't know what you are or who you are but this is my garden and my apple tree and my day bed so stay away!...........Please!

Dondo thinking it might be well to be polite and show good manners.

At this point the noise came again Aaaawoooooo followed by a gentle woof or wuph! Dondo raised an eyebrow then took off to gallop around the garden fence just to check that the noise wasn't coming from inside the garden.

As Dondo passed the white picket front gate Dondo stopped and looked and looked and there on the other side of the gate was the smallest dog Dondo had ever seen.

A white fluffy ball of fluff and more fluff you couldn't tell where the dog began and the tail finished there were no eyes and no nose just huge ball of fluff.

In dog barky language Dondo said sternly, "who are you?" The white fluff ball on the other side of the fence just said "wuph" a sad soggy "wuph" too.

Dondo said what are you? As Dondo had never seen anything like this before, the fluffy dog said "I is lost, I don't know my ways back home, do you know where I lives", "I definitely do not!" replied Dondo sternly waggling a tail.

Dondo marched up and down the line of the white fence with a nose held high in the air and ears twitching furiously making sure the fluffy ball was aware that this was Dondo's patch and no other dog will pass.

Dondo asked "what is your name?" "Snowball" the fluffy dog said in barky talk. "And what sort of a dog's name is that?" Dondo scoffed "Is it a cat's name?"

The fluffy ball then said in clear barky talk,

"I is no cat, I is a dog and a ruff dog too",

The white fluffy snowball started to bark "rrrraagght rrrraagght rrrraagght!" Just to prove the point, it went on and on and on!

"SSSSSSSSTOP Barking!" Said Dondo in a loud barky voice,

Dondo had to say it four or five times to make himself heard they both were making quiet a racket, at that Dondo's Lady owner came down the garden shouting at Dondo, " Dondo Dondo "!

What on earth is going on young Dondo, why are you"….then she stopped and looked down at the little ball of fluff, "oh my, oh my" she said "now who might you be"?

She bent down and picked up the little fluffy dog and held her in her arms stroking the little trembling dog.

"Aren't you a little cutie, come along with me she said ill find you a drink and a biscuit" Said the Lady.

"No No No!" thought Dondo "not my Biscuit, please don't eat my biscuit!"

Oh no, Dondo thought "not my personal water bowl either",

Dondo followed very close behind as the three of them made their way up the long long garden to the house.

The Lady took the tiny fluffy dog to the kitchen and gave him a biscuit - "freshly made that afternoon, then she put the little dog down next to the water bowl, immediately the little dog began to drink, and drink and drink the little dog must be about ready to burst!

Dondo looked on, that's my biscuit and that's my water bowl he pondered, Dondo turned looked very disappointed and felt quiet sad and went back into the garden to settle under the apple tree. Crossing paws and resting his chin on them, Dondo watched the kitchen door.

The Lady owner came down into the garden and said good dog Dondo you saved your little friend and made a new friend. Well done Dondo you are a good dog…as she stroked him and patted his head……. I think you are a magnificent dog my lovely Dondo and then the owner gave Dondo two biscuits, freshly made that afternoon.

Dondo felt he was losing control of his tail again! Oh no! It was twitching! Oh no! and sure enough as he tucked into the biscuits a happy tail began to wagg madly again. Dondo felt a little pleased that this new friend has got Dondo two biscuits instead of the normal one.

Soon after Dondo had cleaned up all the tiniest biscuit crumbs and saw the little fluffy dog sat on the doorstep looking quiet full and a little sleepy, Dondo could hear the Lady owner on the tephalone, she often used a tephalone to talk, talk to herself so he thought.

But on this occasion she was reporting the little lost dog to the local policeman.

She told the local policeman the little dog had no collar or tag with any information on it, hadn't had any food for quite a time and obviously been drinking from puddles, he told her not to worry there had been no reports of a missing dog in the village and that he would pop around later that day.

Snowball came down into the garden sniffing around and looking a little better, the Lady had cleaned the little dog up given it a brush and there were two little brown eyes, the little dog came over to Dondo and said in Barky barks , thank you Dondo, it was a lovely biscuit, Dondo said you're welcome little Snowball.

Dondo was feeling relaxed again and settled into the hollow under the apple tree.

Snowball asked if there was room for two, and settled besides Dondo, they both snoozed under the branches of the apple tree as the breeze wafted them both off to sleep, Dondo was dreaming of Rabbits and a good old chase and Snowball was dreaming of meat pie which had been seen going into the oven.

Later on, both were startled by the squeak of an old bicycle wheel coming down the lane, they both went over to look who or what was coming towards the old house through the white fence,

The Lady came out to greet PC Wobblebelly the policeman, he leant his bicycle against the fence and came into the garden and sat down with a cup of tea and ....

Biscuits! , "Freshly made that afternoon".

Both dogs settled back into the hollow under the apple tree and with one eye open each spying the biscuit situation a few feet away.

The Lady and the policeman continued to talk about the little dog, the policeman removed his hat, he said they had no reports of any lost dogs in the village or nearby, certainly non matching the description given by the Lady, oh dear she said well what do we do with it.

The policeman looked around and said "well Dondo seems to have the situation under control."

"Yes" the Lady said "Dondo is a magnificent dog".

The policemen asked "What are you going to call the little dog?

"It can only be Snowball" she said,

The policeman smiled and agreed as he dunked another of the delicious biscuits in his cup of very sweet tea and said "that's a perfect name".

He turned to Dondo and said "well-done Dondo" and held a bit of a biscuit out for him.

Dondo sat up and went over, very gently took the biscuit and went back to where Snowball was sat under the apple tree and shared the treat with little Snowball. "Well I never" said the policeman "Dondo really is a magnificent Dog". The Lady sat and drank her cup of tea looking very proud.

During that long summer Dondo and Snowball enjoyed the warmth of the summer months under their apple tree and loved nothing better than a dreamy snooze of rabbit chasing followed by biscuits and meat pie for tea. Snuggles on the big feather bed, and each other's friendship.

It was agreed by all that Snowball would stay at the house for as long as needed and would looked after by the old Lady and "Dondo the Magnificent".

Snowball and Dondo in time became firm friends and loved to wallow and snooze under the apple tree in the long long garden of the old house in the Leafy Lane.

This is where Dondo would dream about chasing rabbits, his new friend Snowball with the smallest legs would dream about trying to keep up with Dondo the Magnificent.

Of course Dogs are only interested in two things, did you

guess what they are?   "Biscuits
baked freshly that afternoon,
Meat pies…… and sleeping!
Oops that's three things!!

The Wonderful Adventures of

Dondo the Magnificent

Second Story

Ducks

So one day in the leafy garden in the old
cottage at the bottom of the lane, Dondo and
his new friend Snowball slept almost

peacefully, wafting buzzy bee's away with the flick of a wonky ear, under the dappled branches of the apple tree they both had come to love so much.

The comforting wafting smells of freshly cooked biscuits from the cottage kitchen made the noses on the two pals wet and twitchy as they slept and both quietly snoring. Two wet noses were already sniffing the air as they dreamed their favourite dreams of chasing biscuit flavoured rabbits.

The Lady of the old cottage had just finished a new tray of biscuits, when the "squeak, squeak, squeak" of an old bicycle wheel made its way right into Dondo ears, up Dondo jumped and let out his nervous bark. Standing up to attention nose pointing in the direction of the strange squeaking almost screeching sound his wonky ear was twitching furiously.

Snowball was in a deep comfortable sleepy enjoyable snooze and he gave out a gruffy huffy bark too, more in that he was miffed that his lovely comfortable dreamy sleep had been disturbed, not by the squeaky screechy wheel but more of Dondo's alarming bark… "At" the squeaky screechy wheel.

The squeak came from the front wheel of the village policeman, PC Wobblebelly, well that's what everyone in the village knew him by. He didn't mind too much and was a friendly jolly policeman.

His real name was PC William Warberry and "PC Wobblebelly" was his nickname.

You see, PC Wobblebelly was quite fond of the biscuits cooked every day by the Lady of the cottage, for she made the best biscuits in the village and, she made them fresh every day to her own special recipe.

The recipe was not really a secret one, it was a special one, she never told anyone what was in her biscuits, the only soul that knew was Dondo, and he listened often as she told him and him alone what was in the special fresh daily biscuits.

He of course would sit there and listen with one ear up and one ear down, as we all know Dondo had his well-known wonky ear and his love of biscuits.

PC Wobblebelly leant his bike on the white picket fence next to the garden gate "tingled" his bell and knocked three times on the gate post to get the attention of the Lady of the cottage, she came to the door and waved to him with a tea towel.

He opened the gate and stepped into the garden to be met by Dondo and little Snowball, both dogs having a good sniff of PC Wobblebelly's big shiny boots.

"Hello - Good afternoon" he bellowed across the garden,

"And good afternoon to you Bill" Perfect timing, she replied,

Dondo and Snowball enjoyed a good ruffle of their furry coats from PC Wobblebelly as he made his way through the garden gate.

"Hello you two" he whispered. Of all the dogs in the village of which there were 23 these two were his favourite, he always had a nice welcome from them.

They made their way across the grass to the table and chairs set out in front of the cottage, PC Wobblebelly removed his police helmet and loosened the top button of his smart and clean police uniform tunic.

"It is a warm day" he said,

"It is a lovely day Bill", replied the Lady, "please take a seat and make yourself comfortable".

"How have you been today?" Asked the Lady,

"Have you been busy?"

He took a breath and loosened his tie, then said;

"Yes it is, you know that it is always busy in our village" rolling his eyes and chuckling.

The Lady poured two cups of piping hot tea, with two dogs at her feet looking hopeful, She pushed forward a plate of her freshly cooked biscuits towards PC Wobblebelly,

"Oh" he said "biscuits!" as he stirred in 3 spoonful's of sugar into his tea.

PC Wobblebelly's eyes were popping with a big smile, as the biscuits were his favourite.

After all, he called in for a cup of tea a few times a week, he always said "Well of course, tea is too wet without a biscuit." It was the policeman's little joke.

"They are just out of the oven Bill so toasty hot! Mind your mouth" the Lady said.

Dondo looked up, at the plate of hot fresh tasty biscuits, they do look really delicious and smell even more so, thought Dondo! And so did little Snowball licking his lips in agreement in the hope of a few delicious crumbs.

And so did PC Wobblebelly. "Of course, you see, tea is too wet without a biscuit." he said.

"So Bill, tell us, what news do you have for us today?" Asked the Lady.

"Well you won't believe this" he said picking up his first biscuit, you know the old village pond at the end of the lane" said PC Wobblebelly as his pushed another half of a biscuit in the corner of his mouth, "the one with the big willow tree"

"Yes" said the Lady.

"Well the duck there has 10 eggs on her nest".

"Really" said the Lady "isn't that wonderful".

"We must take a walk down there and have a look when the little ones come along shall we Dondo?"

The Lady lovingly patted Dondo on the head.

Dondo held his head to one side then the other as he twitched his wonky ear with a quizzical look on his face. Dondo didn't know what a "dulck" was?

"They should be hatching any day soon I would guess" said PC Wobblebelly, as he pushed another biscuit into his mouth and slurping a big mouthful of very sweet tea from the tea cup.

"Oh well when you do see them Bill please let me know I'd love to see the little darlings" said the Lady.

"I will" said PC Wobblebelly, "they are well hidden in the reeds though, so please be careful."

"But I must warn you, please keep your dogs on a lead as we don't want to scare the family of ducks away."

"With a friendly wagg of his finger and a smile, PC Wobblebelly said to Dondo and Snowball   "and no loud barking boys, shushsh please"

"Oh don't worry Bill; Dondo and Snowball love to walk with me down the lane through the buttercup field, when we get to the end I do always put the two boys on a lead" Said the Lady.

"Very wise" said the Policeman.

"As soon as I know they are hatched and well, I will pop by and let you know" He said.

"That would be really nice Bill, thank you that is kind" said the Lady.

"Thank you for the tea and biscuits" said the Policeman as he stood up, "it was delicious".

At that Dondo pricked up his ears and sat up, the policeman broke a biscuit in two and offered it to Dondo and Snowball.

"Paw"! Said the policeman sternly and both dogs offered a little paw in return for the half biscuits "good boys" said PC Wobblebelly and gently patted them on the head.

The policemen and the Lady talked for a while and then it was time for the policemen to return back to his duties, he thanked the Lady again for his tea and biscuits, " you are very kind" he said, he straightened his tie and made his way to the garden gate to make his way off on his old but rusty and reliable squeaky wheeled bicycle.

Dondo and Snowball returned to the warm dappled hollow under the apple tree and made their way into some lovely gentle dreams about ducklings, whatever they were; and sleepy dreams of chasing biscuit flavoured rabbits as the noise of the squeaky bicycle slowly disappeared down the lane and the apple tree through dappled sunlight wafted its leaves in the breeze.

Dondo thought to himself that this was the most perfect place to be with Snowball his best friend, any day.

A few days later the squeaky wheel returned, with a PC Wobblebelly puffing and panting as he pedalled his bicycle hard up the gentle slope leading to the cottage where Dondo and Snowball lived. He came to the gate and gave the now normal "Hello - Good Morning", the Lady of the cottage came out to meet him.

"Im afraid you are too early Bill, the Biscuits are not in the oven yet", she said as she made her way down the grassy garden towards the gate. The two dogs following her close behind.

"Oh please don't worry I've not made my way up here just for your delicious biscuits today,

I have some exciting news for you", "the chicks are here!"

He had a big smile on his face as if he was really excited to pass on the good news of the new arrivals.

"Well done Bill" the Lady said, "that is good news", "Im taking the boys for a walk in a short while we will have a look to see if we can say hello to the new village resident's".

The policemen turned his bicycle around and made his way back down the lane waving cheerio as he went off.

"Come on boys a quick lunch then we can go to see some new friends" said the Lady, Dondo and snowball were close behind and only concentrating on that one word.......Lunch!, which to the two dogs sounded just like "FOOD"

After Lunch the two dogs sat at the garden gate waiting to be let out to start their walk, "Sit boys" said the Lady, "walk with me" she instructed them, and as Dondo walked with the Lady, Snowball followed the Lady and Dondo close behind.

Leafy lane was a quiet place narrow with high hedges and lots of shady trees lining each side, the breeze would gently waft the cow parsley and dock leaves in the breeze, this was one of the Lady's best times of the day as she loved leafy lane and her peaceful walk along it with her two loyal companions Dondo and Snowball.

About half way down Leafy Lane there is a style and a farmer's gate, this leads into a meadow of poppies, wild flowers and buttercups, a wash of golden yellow met their eyes, and it was a splendid sight indeed.

The two dogs knew their way into the meadow and jumped through the gaps in the farmer's gate as the Lady stepped through and over the style. "Off you go" she called as they waited for her instruction and the two pals ran off excitedly kicking their heels as they went speeding through the buttercups and poppy's and off along the track, the Lady strolled behind the boys as the skylarks twittered above their heads, Snowball was trying to keep up with Dondo, as Dondo quiet clearly had the longest legs and Snowball the shortest ones.

At the end of the track was another much smaller gate, both dogs sat there waiting for the Lady as they did both dogs were panting with long tongues out as they cooled off on the warm afternoon following their run through the buttercup fields. "You are good Boys" the Lady said as she approached them. She lent down and put their dog leads on as she passed through the gate back on to the end of Leafy Lane.

Opposite the end of the Lane was the old red post box, the Lady had with her two letters, one for her sister who lived in France and one for her son who lived a long way from Leafy Lane near London , she often wrote to them at the same time and shared to each the same news. The Lady walked across the road and posted her letters into the red letterbox the dogs following safely on their leads.

As she turned around she heard a voice from across the pond "Hello - there, good afternoon", there sat on a bench next to the village pond was her friend the policeman PC Wobblebelly, he was sitting there very still, besides him was his old lunch box, it was open and he was eating his sandwich, he gestured the Lady to join him and held a finger up to his lips, "shussssh" he said quietly.

The Lady and the two dogs made their way over to him and sat bedsides him, he took the finger from his lips and pointed towards the water in the pond and there close to the reeds was the mother Mallard duck, she was all plump and proudly leading 10 little fluffy chick's all in a line behind her, swimming around the pond in single file closely following her.

The little chicks were chirping away and making quiet a lot of noise, every now and then the Mother Duck would turn and swim in another direction and quack a little at the ducklings to make sure they didn't wander off and so they kept on following Mum. It was a quiet quack that in duck language probably meant "Follow me children, this way please"

Dondo and Snowball were both fascinated as they has never seen such a thing like this before. Dondo thought "ah ha so these are dulcklings then" his ears twitching as he followed the little ones up and down the pond.

The Lady, the Policeman, Dondo and Snowball all sat together and watched speechless as the parade of ducks circled the pond round and round in front of them.

"Isn't it wonderful Bill" said the Lady,

"All this new life, it is just the best treat to see it."

"It is indeed a wonderful treat" the policeman said with a muffled voice, he was trying to get yet another sausage roll into his mouth quietly before the two dogs could see him, but too late.

Detective Dondo's well trained nose was already on the case and so was the nose of his partner 'Sergeant Snowball', "hello hello" "oh dear ... oh dear, what have we here?" thought Dondo ... "Osage rollz hmm! - Case solved!!

PC Wobblebelly has been rumbled, before he knew it the policeman had two dogs at his feet both looking as if they had not seen a sausage roll before in their lives …. Ever!

And of course, as dogs do, they were giving him that special look.

PC Wobblebelly smiled at them, he knew what they wanted, he reached into his lunch box and pulled out one more sausage roll, the one that he had saved for his two little pals, he broke it in two and offered it to the dogs in return for a paw from each of them, as they munched on the sausage rolls he gave them both a pat on the head, with his spare hand he threw the flaky crumbs onto the water for the ducks to peck at.

At once! and with one swift acrobatic move Snowball leaped into the air almost summersaulting, he was after the crumbs, obviously thinking the flaky crumbs was another sausage roll! He moved as if he was in slow motion through the air past the policeman's bicycle towards the pond.

Sploshhhsshhh!! Into the water he fell, sending a big wave across the pond.

Under the water he went, rolling and tumbling into the pond.

Dondo stood up and couldn't believe his eyes, all around the pond was chaos, Snowball was paddling in circles near the bank trying to get out, but he kept sinking beneath the water.

Dondo was trying to reach his pal and pull him out, in and out of the reeds Dondo searched desperately in and out of the reeds again to find his little muddy white friend.

The Lady called to Snowball as he tumbled over and over in the water, what had become clear was that Snowball couldn't swim! The little dog was panicking!!

"Oh My Oh My" said the Lady "what a bothersome thing" Snowball, Snowball" she shouted in hope he would hear her and swim towards her voice in her direction.

All of a sudden Dondo made a big hero leap across the reeds into the water with a big splash, he surface from beneath the dirty water and swam towards snowball, this churned up the dirty smelly pond water as they struggled.

Dondo grabbed snowball by his collar with his teeth and turned around making a strong swim towards the bank of the pond.

"Nearly there Snowball" Dondo growled, "I hope so, hurry Dondo I don't think I can swim" whimpered snowball,

At last they made it to the bankside, PC Wobblebelly stooped down and grabbed snowball by the scruff of his neck and landed him on the grass next to the bench.

Dondo dragged himself out of the water and both dogs gave the biggest muddy wet shake of their coats soaking PC Wobblebelly and the Lady at the same time from top to toe with dark brown smelly muddy pond water.

"Well, I thank you for that" said the policeman, as he wiped his jacket.

"Oh I am so sorry Bill" said the Lady

"Bill you are covered in muddy water you will need your uniform cleaning"

"Let us not worry about that now" said PC Wobblebelly with a very concerned frown on his face, "look" he said pointing to the pond.

The Lady, Dondo, and shivering Snowball turned around, the water of the pond was dark and brown with smelly old mud churned up by Snowball and Dondo sploshing about, but the worse thing was….

The mother Duck and her Ducking's had gone!!

"Oh no! "Oh no!" said the Lady she was really upset

"Oh no!!!" what have we done "cried the Lady.

"This is terrible" she said "oh no, where have they gone"?

PC Wobblebelly had walked further long the bank his jacket and hat dripping with the smelly muddy water.

He came back and said "Im sorry, there is no sign of them"

"Oh Dear Bill this is a shame"

After a few minutes the water in the pond settled down, the Lady and the policemen sat down, they didn't speak a word and just sat there in shock looking at the brown water in the pond.

They really couldn't believe it. They were feeling so sad.

Dondo and Snowball were very quiet, something was telling them something really bad had happened, they were not too sure if it had something to do with them. Snowball was feeling very sad and soggy he knew it was something to do with him and a sausage roll.

All of a sudden Dondo's wonky ear twitched, then it twitched again, "what can you hear Dondo?" Said the Lady, She knew that if Dondo's wonky ear starts to twitch he is hearing something humans can't.

Dondo stood up and his ear twitched again!
What could it be?

Dondo ran around the pond to almost the far
side, he was weaving in and out of the reeds,
the Lady and PC Wobblebelly looked on
Snowball was hiding behind the Lady.

Dondo barked and out of the reeds flew
Mother Duck. She fluttered around the
bottom end of the pond and landed quiet near
to the Lady and PC Wobblebelly. Oh thank
goodness she is ok said the Lady.

The Policeman was still concerned about the
little ones, the ducklings. Where could they
be?

Dondo continued to search for the thing his
ears had been telling him, he had heard a little
chirp and followed his nose and of course his
wonky ear in the direction of the chirping.

Pretty soon from behind the rushes he popped in and gently with his lips lifted out a little duckling, he bought it back the side of the pond where the Lady was sitting. He dropped the duckling near to the Mother duck and it scurried quickly across the grass to be reunited with its Mum.

Dondo ran off again to the other side of the pond again he returned, this time with two little ducklings.

PC Wobblebelly and the Lady called to Dondo, "good boy Dondo find the others"

Dondo slowly worked his way around the pond coming back with a little duckling, one or two each time.

After a time Dondo couldn't find anymore and went back and sat by the Lady, she said "well done my boy you are a magnificent dog" patting him on the head.

We have a problem said PC Wobblebelly, "what's the matter asked the Lady", well he said im sure we had 10 ducklings, we now only have ......9.

Oh my word said the Lady, "Dondo, Snowball off you go boys find the little one"

The boys ran off and went round the pond in opposite directions, in and out of the bushes and reeds and rushes around the pond they went, but still no sign of the lost duckling,

Then Dondo heard something again and his wonky ear started to twitch and twitch it did. He pointed his nose in the direction of the last little noise he had heard.

In the middle of the pond was a small island and on it was a little house, Dondo was convinced he had heard the chirp coming from inside the little house, but he needed help to get there.

Dondo ran around the pond and growled quietly at Snowball, "I need help" he growled.

Snowball immediately knew what Dondo needed, the pair rushed to the other side of the pond where Snowball climbed on the back of Dondo.

"My word "said the policeman lifting his helmet and scratching his head as the two dogs went into action!

Splosh into the smelly brown pond they went, Snowball riding high on Dondo's back across the pond, when they reached the little island Snowball leaped off,

He scrambled up the bank onto the little island and went for a look around the back of the island through the reeds, then inside the little house sniffing the ground as he went, Dondo thought they were on to something.

The Lady and the Policemen held their breath , ...then....... miraculously a few seconds later Snowball came out of the little house gripping the little lost ducking, the ducking was wriggling and chirping away shouting for its mother.

Quickly Snowball and the chick scrambled down the bank and jumped aboard Dondo's back and the three of them made their way for a long swim back to the bank, it was a good job Dondo was a good swimmer!

Snowball jumped off still with his little recued chick in his lips, he came over to the place where the mother duck and the other 9 chicks were fussing about and dropped the lost ducking to its mother at her feet. She looked so relieved the little one was safe again.

Dondo looked at Snowball he gruffed a "Well done Snowball - good work"

Snowball yapped back to Dondo "Good work too Dondo"

The Mother duck looked at Snowball and Dondo and quacked a "Thank you boys" In Duck talk of course.

PC Wobblebelly and the Lady were trying to count the chicks which was proving difficult as they were running around the mother duck, all of the little ones so excited to be back with their Mum.

"456 7" Oh lost count" he said start again "56789 and 10 all present and correct" said PC Wobblebelly.

"Thank goodness for that said the Lady", "what an afternoon" she said.

"Certainly and eventful one my dear " said the policeman lifting his hat to scratch his

head as he couldn't believe what had
happened all in a few minutes.

The Lady and the policemen turned to
Snowball and Dondo, "well you two really
made a difference this afternoon" said pc
Wobblebelly, "well done boys, what a team,
well done Snowball and well done Dondo -
you're both Magnificent".

Within a few minutes the Duck had taken her
little ones onto the pond again, pretty soon
the little ones had started to follow Mum
chirping away in unison in a line,

Peace had returned to the pond.

The Lady and PC Wobblebelly and the dogs
made their way to the Police Station office
where PC Wobblebelly was able to put on his
spare jacket, the Lady took his dirty and

smelly jacket home as she had promised to clean it.

Dondo and Snowball walked with the Lady down Leafy lane toward the cottage passing through the meadow full of yellow golden buttercups, the Skylarks twittering above their heads again, there the two pals rushed off and waited for the Lady to arrive at the style and famers gate, at the other end of the field, then on a short stroll to the cottage where the apple tree and the hollow beneath welcomed them for a sleep before supper.

"What a busy afternoon boys" said the Lady, as she put her jacket down on the chair in her kitchen and leant her walking stick against the wall," but I am very proud of what you have done today. I think an extra bit of pie each is in order don't you?"

Both dogs looked at each other secretly pleased with the extra pie news! It would surely be a delicious end to the busy day.

Dondo and Snowball were now quiet tired, they had really had a special eventful day, one from where their dreams of rescuing tiny ducklings and swimming in the pond took them away into a deep sleep whilst they waited for a meat pie supper, drifting off into a warm comfy snooze was for the two dogs no better place. The smell of meat pies and biscuits wafted across the garden perfect for dog's noses.

The hollow under the apple tree was Dondo's best dreaming place and one he loved to share with Snowball a real best friend and companion.

"This is just the perfect place to be" he thought, being very proud that he was

Dondo the Magnificent.

The Wonderful Adventures of

Story Three

Dondo the Magnificent

Harriet and Horace, Hannah Henry Hugo and spike, came for tea!

One late September on a Thursday afternoon in the Leafy Lane cottage garden, Dondo the Magnificent was coming out of the cottage down the steps having gone inside to see if the extra big meaty meat and gravy pie was anywhere near ready.

Dondo's well trained nose told him it wasn't far off being ready and he certainly had hoped that it was. Having got in the way and under the feet of the Lady who lived in the cottage in Leafy Lane, he had been shooed back into the garden.

"Off you go Dondo, good Boy" the Lady said" Thursday pie is not ready yet"

It had been a warm day in September and the snoozing and sleeping under the apple tree in the dappled sunlight had been exceptionally good.

Apart from that is, the occasional apple dropping off the apple tree, dislodged by the breeze and sometimes catching Dondo on the nose with an unwelcome bump!, waking him from a dream with a bit of a start!!!

Dondo was disappointed that the big meaty meat pie was a little time away from being ready, deliciously warm with lashings of gravy the thought of it was making him extra hungry, as it was his favourite variety the Lady called it "Thursday pie".

Dondo had popped into the garden to wake up his best friend Snowball who was still snoring away under the apple tree. Snowball was busy dreaming of rabbits and chasing the especially tasty biscuit flavoured ones.

Out of the corner of Dondo's eye he saw something move under the hedge, he stood very still and at the same time heard a little tiny squeak. He looked again and all he could see was a few brown spikey balls which he had thought had dropped off the nearby tree.

Dondo's wonky ear was revolving like a radar trying to locate where or what the sound was and where it was coming from.

Snowball was stretching as he was waking up his sleepy head, yawning happily, but with a quizzical look on his face wondering what on earth Dondo was doing, was his friend playing a game of statues or making himself into a new type of very unusual garden table? He was keeping very very still.

Again, there is was, Dondo and this time Snowball too had heard the tiny little squeak, neither Snowball nor Dondo could see where exactly it was coming from, they just couldn't work it out. It did seem that it was coming from the direction of the rocky path next to the big hedge.

Slowly the two friends lowered their noses closer to the ground, like detective dogs they moved towards the little brown balls of spiky leaves, Dondo hadn't seen anything like them before, Snowball crept forwards under the shadow of Dondo's long legs, which was easy as he was so small.

Carefully the two friends moved closer and closer still. They could see that there was one big ball and some smaller tiny brown balls.

"Take care" Dondo gruffed to Snowball in doggy language.

"I will" grumbled Snowball, being so small he was a little more worried than his best friend Dondo at this strange sight. Closer and closer they got then all of a sudden a bigger squeak came from the big brown ball, SQUEAK!!!! Dondo leaped back, Snowball scurried back too. Then all the little brown balls all at once started tiny little squeaks, Squeak! Squeak! Squeak! Squeak! Squeak! Squeak!!!!

Dondo was amazed and at the same time spooked by the noise, Little Snowball ran around and around almost chasing his own tail trying to make some sense of what these tiny balls were.

Then Dondo not wanting this noise to go on any longer let out his best and most magnificent "ruffty tuffty gruffy" bark "Growlfff"!................ Then it all was silent again. Dondo Looked at Snowball they both raised an eyebrow "how very strange" they thought.

The door of the cottage opened and the Lady said come on boys there is some meaty meat pie here for you, both dogs looked at the Lady on the cottage doorway, then looked again!

Dondo and Snowball could hardly believe their eyes....as they looked the balls started to unravel and become little animals scurrying around, one was bigger than the others and seemed to be the Mum ...or Dad.

The little ones were following Mum or Dad and squeaking at the top of their little voices, Dondo was a wise old dog and in his past he had learnt to use a sort of language that used his paws his nose, his eyebrows and of course his wonky ear, he asked the big ball......what are you?

Then, the door of the cottage opened again, the Lady called "come on boys the pie is getting cold", Dondo looked at the Lady and gave a little bark. The Lady could see they were looking at something and started her way across the garden,

"What is it Dondo"? The Lady asked,

She made her way towards Dondo and Snowball on the garden path, "what is i………..oh" as she stopped in her tracks "Oh my word"! "Hello Mr Hedgehog, How lovely to see you". The Lady said to the little Hedgehog.

Dondo twitched his wonky ear and looked at Snowball he whispered under his breath 'in doggie language to Snowball' "Hey Snowy, Hedgebog? What's a Hedgebog?"

Snowball whispered back in doggie language "you need to get that wonky ear fixed, she said Hedgehog not Hedgebog"

Well what's a Hedgehog then, Dondo whispered to Snowball,

"I don't know Dondo I've never seen one have I?" snapped Snowball, getting a little impatient with Dondo.

The Lady said "this little lot look hungry to me", you boys wait here I'll go and get then something from the kitchen".

When the Lady returned she had two saucers in her hands, one had some mushed up 'Thursday pie' and the other has some milk, as soon as she put them down the little hedgehogs circled the saucer and started lapping the milk furiously. They all looked so thirsty.

Look at that Snowball, they were very thirsty and hungry, Dondo nudged the saucer with the Thursday Pie towards the big Hedgehog, he came slowly to the saucer and said "thank you", Dondo replied "you're welcome".

The Lady, Dondo and Snowball waited for a few minutes just to watch the little family tuck into the milk and Thursday Pie, then a loud whistling sound came from the kitchen, it was the kettle boiling.

Come on boys let's leave them to eat and we will get our pie too, at that Dondo and Snowball followed the Lady back to the kitchen where the two friends ate lovely Thursday pie with lashings of warm tasty meaty pie and some carrots which were Dondo's favourite veggie, Snowball was getting quiet fond of them too.

With a satisfying slurp Dondo cleaned off his dish, it looked spotless, he could almost see his face in the bottom of the shiny dish, a sure sign to the Lady that Dondo appreciated her delicious pies.

Snowball was still eating his slice of Thursday pie, licking his lips between every mouthful and taking his time loving every mouthful, the pie and the tasty gravy and carrots were truly delicious, so he was taking his time to savour every morsel, and thinking how lucky he was to be in such a lovely home.

Dondo had wandered over to the window to see if the little hedgehogs were still there. He could see they were circled around the two saucers, he looked at the Lady,

She said "oh go on Dondo go and see your new friends",

Dondo poked his nose at the door and pushed it open, off he trotted with a waggley tail into the garden and down the path by the big hedge.

When he got the place where the little family was eating he sat patiently, the big hedgehog came over and said thank you for my food and thank you for the drink for my children. Dondo signalled with his special way of talking "you are very welcome"

What is your name asked Dondo, the big hedgehog replied I am Horace, these are three of my children, Hannah, Henry and Hugo.

Dondo asked where you were going when you come into our garden.

Well we have had a bit of a bad time said the hedgehog, I have lost my wife Harriet and my other son Spike, we were out for a worm picnic and we were separated when a big bicycle came past us as we crossed the road. I've not seen her since yesterday. I am very worried and my children are extremely upset.

We came into your garden hoping that h an s had come for safety here.

Dondo looked shocked, and sad that the little family were is such distress.

The hedgehog said he had desperately searched for them, in the lane, on the big buttercup field and over the old golf course they searched all night but sadly no luck. He looked so glum and sad.

Just at that time Dondo's wonky ear twitched! Approaching came the sound of another familiar squeak squeak! It was PC Wobblebelly's police bike!

As the squeaky bicycle approached and got louder all of the hedgehogs vanished and rolled up into a ball under the hedge. It was just like they had magically disappeared. They had huddled together and were completely out of sight.

Dondo turned to watch the policemen get off his bike and lean it against the fence, he shouted a big Heeello! and wandered onto the garden giving Dondo a pat on the head as he passed towards the Kitchen door, Dondo heard him knock on the door and the Lady opening it, "

"Hello Bill "she said "nice to see you",

"Hello" said PC Wobblebelly "I was just passing so I thought I would check you and the dogs are OK."

"Yes thank you Bill" the Lady turned to fill the kettle again to make a fresh pot of tea, as she did she smiled and rolled her eyes, she really didn't mind.

"We are all fine, you are just in time for a slice of Thursday Pie and I think there is a last cup of tea in the teapot and Im making a fresh one too."

"Oh really" said PC Wobblebelly "are you sure? "My timing seems to be just right" Snowball was just finishing his dinner and looked up, and rolled his eyes too, PC Wobblebelly was always here on a Thursday evening mainly because of that" "Thursday Pie""!!!

As PC Wobblebelly settled down at the table, Snowball licked his lips and went to sit on his bed in the kitchen by the window so he could see Dondo and the hedgehog family across the garden.

So How has today been in the busy world of policing asked the Lady as she passed to him a slice of the famous and delicious Thursday Pie, Well he said it has been quiet overall nothing serious to report thank goodness. He tucked into the pie and rook a long slurp of his cup of tea/

All good at the pond the little family of ducklings has now flown the nest and the pond is again fairly quiet.

I came down to check on the cricket ground yesterday and nearly had an accident.

Oh no Bill why what happened, the Lady asked and was concerned.

Well as I turned by the style gate into the buttercup field just passed the bend in the road there was a family of Hedgehogs of all things crossing the road in a big line, I managed to swerve and miss did them It sent one lot across the road and a couple of them were set into the gully,

The Lady asked if he had stopped.

"I didn't stop as they seemed to be alright they ran away.

 Hmmm nom this pie is very good he said with his mouth full and bulging as he took another loud slurp of his tea. "Delicious" he said under his breath.

Snowball was listening close by and had pricked his ears up. He overheard the Policemen's story, Snowball didn't understand all of the human words, but Snowball thought it odd that Hedgehogs were by the buttercup field, he thought Dondo should know immediately.

Snowball bumped the kitchen door open made his way down the wooden steps and into the garden He found Dondo still by the hedge. "I need to tell you something Dondo" said Snowball in the dog language.

The policeman saw some other hedgehogs near the buttercup field yesterday - Lady upset"

Both of Dondo's ears stood straight up!

"How you know this Snowball?" Dondo asked.

Policemen eating pie told Lady!

"Ok" Dondo replied

Dondo turned to the Hedgehog who was still in a big ball under the hedge, Dondo said "I need to ask you something", the hedgehog unravelled himself, He said in a frightened voice "has it gone yet?

Has what gone? Asked Dondo.

"The Big Squeaky Machine thing."

Dondo understood now what has frightened the hedgehogs and sent them under the big hedge.

If Snowballs story was right then they might be able to help. Dondo turned and ran to the cottage and into the kitchen.

The Lady looked startled a Dondo rushed in, he was waggling his tail furiously barking and pulling at the Lady's apron. Clearly he thought something was very important for her to see.

"Dondo shush with that barking, what on earth is it boy"? He gently pulled her to the door, she followed Dondo shouting back to the Kitchen door where PC Wobblebelly was still sat munching at the pie,

"I will just be a minute Bill carry on"

Dondo was frantic and was pulling the Lady towards the gate, ok Dondo not so fast what is it boy.

Dondo pointed his nose at the hedgehogs under the big hedge, they were starting to come out again he then pointed up the lane towards the gate into the big buttercup field.

"Ok" the Lady said realising Dondo had something important to tell her, she looked across at the hedgehogs and said "is it something to do with the hedgehog family?"

Dondo ran round and round in circles, barking and jumping as if to say "yes come on come on this way follow me!" Snowball joined and was copying Dondo, "Ok Ok boys, let me come with you"

The made their way into leafy lane Dondo was skipping ahead then turned to make sure the Lady was following, as they got to the gate into buttercup field Dondo started sniffing the ground joined by Snowball.

They sniffed and went left and right crossing the pathway into the field, Dondo looked at Snowball and said in doggie language, "you go to the left and I'll go to the right". As they did in a few moments' PC Wobblebelly had caught up with them, "what in earth is the matter?" He puffed.

"Dondo and snowball are being detectives again I fear!" The Lady laughed a little chuckle.

Dondo stopped in his tracks and picked up a scent trail his tail was straight up in the air and his nose was right into the buttercups and wildflowers ploughing a track through the undergrowth.

He continued ahead as the Lady and PC Wobblebelly followed. Snowball joined Dondo as it was clear Dondo was on to something. Overhead the skylarks were chirping away busily in the sky, Dondo looked up and saw one of them swooping towards the back of the field.

He followed their directions, as they seemed to be telling him there was something there.

There were some old logs ahead, Dondo slowed right down, his nose even closer to the ground, as he got closer, he did, and he heard a tiny squeak, very faint but definitely a squeak, coming from the direction of the logs a few feet away.

Dondo looked around at the Lady, he gestured that there as something in the pile of logs, the Lady being unsure of what it might be asked Dondo, "what is it boy"?

Dondo pointed with his body from the tip of his tail to the tip of his nose at the log pile again.

The Lady looked and looked all around but couldn't see anything,

Then the little squeak came again, it was very feint and whatever it was sounded frightened.

"I heard it" she said, she started to remove the top few smaller logs from the pile, and there hidden in the log pile covered with long grass were two spiky balls, they looked like they were wet and pretty cold.

More hedgehogs Dondo the Lady asked? What is it with you and hedgehogs today? PC Wobblebelly looked over the Lady's shoulders and said "they look like the ones I saw on the lane yesterday".

"Oh my "said the Lady, "if they are they might be something to do with those hedgehogs in my garden", do you think they are Dondo?" Dondo jumped up and span around again and with his friend snowball was barking together. That to the Lady was a big Yes!

PC Wobblebelly removed his police helmet and they gently rolled the two hedgehogs into the warm comfy hat.

"Come one lets go back to the garden and reunite these two with their family".

Dondo and Snowball followed close behind, they made their way down leafy lane and into the cottage garden.

The policeman and the Lady gently put the spiky balls on the lawn and stepped back, "come on boys keep back and give them some room".

As they did the hedgehogs in the big hedge appeared, they made their way straight to the two balls curled up on the lawn.

Dondo watched as the hedgehog called Horace approached and nudged the biggest of the two balls, it was indeed Harriet his wife and his son little Spike, reunited with her husband and Spike with his brothers and sisters.

"Oh my word" said the Lady, "I think they are all one family," "oh goodness me" said the policeman, "I feel very responsible for all of this as I may have slit them up in the lane yesterday oh dear oh dear. I am sorry, so sorry!"

The Lady made her way to the cottage once more and returned a few minutes later with two more saucers of milk and the leftovers of the Thursday pie mushed up so it would be easy for them to nibble on, she also put a few slices of apple for the little ones.

Dondo settled down with his chin on the grass looking on as the hedgehogs were re acquainted and scurried around obviously pleased and really happy to see each other, in a matter of minutes there was a very happy Horace and Harriet together with their children Hannah, Henry, Hugo, and little Spike.

Snowball sat next to Dondo and said in doggie language, "well done Dondo, another case solved".

"I could not have done it without you Snowy, well done to you too".

The policeman PC Wobblebelly said to the Lady, "well I'm so glad all of this turned out so well, your two dogs are remarkable, such good dogs."

The Lady looked at Dondo with a proud look on her face and smiled fondly at the two of them looking at their new friends and said "Yes they are special, My Dondo is truly a magnificent dog.

The little happy gathering went on for some time, into the evening until PC Wobblebelly said he had to go as he was due on duty at the police station again in a few minutes, he got up and said thanks to the Lady for his supper.

She said "you are always welcome", he dusted his helmet off and made his way to the gate and got on his bike.

As soon as he started to pedal and make his way down Leafy Lane the squeaky old front wheel made its familiar noise known well to Dondo and Snowball "squeak! Squeak! Squeak!, Immediately all of the hedgehogs rolled up into tight balls curling themselves up.

The Lady said to Dondo "yes Dondo I think you were right it was PC Wobblebelly who scared this little family apart, something we all know he didn't mean to do and as he was very sorry we should forgive him" "What do you think Dondo?".

Dondo gruffed in agreement, Snowball made a little bark of approval too.

After a few minutes, the hedgehogs had realised the squeaky front bicycle wheel had gone out of sight and any harm and it was safe for then to come out and happily snuffle around the two saucers left by the Lady.

It was starting to get late and time to look forward to bedtime. The two hedgehogs approached Dondo "Thank you very much for your help today Dondo we don't know how to thank you",

Dondo said "it was my pleasure and I am so pleased you are all back together" "and your friendship is thanks enough."

Snowball said to Dondo, "where are they going to sleep?"

Horace said "do not worry, we will find a place under your big hedge there are some nice leaves to settle into if that's ok?"

"The Lady would not mind" said Dondo "make yourself comfortable, and all of you have a good nights sleeping and rest.

"Thank you indeed" said the hedgehogs, they said good night, turned to go under the hedge with the little ones following in a line across the lawn.

As they disappeared under the hedge it was not long before they could not be seen as they blended into the hedgerow and settled all together for the night on a comfortable bed of leaves.

Dondo yawned and so did Snowball the Lady said "come on boys this is all too much excitement for one day lets go to bed."

The following morning, Dondo was soon to be up and ready for a new day of sleeping and relaxing in his favourite apple tree place, the weather was to be good again and Dondo and Snowball could watch their new friends explore the garden safe from the perils of the leafy lane squeaky bicycles especially those with PC Wobblebelly on them.

Horace came to see Dondo and they talked about the journey they wanted to make to the other side of the cricket pitch, "that's where I grew up said Horace I think it's a good place to bring the little ones up". "That's wonderful" said Dondo "I think it's a good idea".

"Before you go would you like some milk and a biscuit? the biscuits are very good, and the little ones will enjoy them and fill their bellies before you set off" Dondo enquired, Harriet said "that would be lovely" and perhaps Dondo and Snowball could join them.

Dondo went to the cottage kitchen door and saw the Lady was putting a fresh tray of biscuits in the oven. They were smelling so good already.

The Lady seeing Dondo looking at her knew immediately what was on his mind, when the biscuits were ready in a while later she came into the garden and offered 3 saucers of milk and a plate of crushed up biscuits for the hedgehogs and a biscuit each for Snowball and Dondo.

The Lady sat at her favourite garden chair in the shade and continued to read a book she was enjoying, as she looked across the garden on the grass it looked like a real tea party was well under way, tiny hedgehogs scurrying around and two proud parents looking on, of course Dondo and Snowball seemed to be the centre of attention and both boys were loving all the fuss from the little ones.

They all enjoyed a nice time in the garden then it was time for the hedgehogs to make a start on their long journey, Dondo had explained the direction they should take and to watch out for a good place to live on the far side of the cricket ground where there was a good wood and some nice hedges to live under, he thought they would be very happy and safe there.

Although he was a little sad to see then go, he knew they would be fine.

So, as the sun was setting again, they went through the white picket gate, the family of six little hedgehogs and hoglets set off.

Along the edge of the leafy lane they scurried in and out of the grassy banks and verges full of clover, and down to the tuning where the cricket ground lay ahead of them. Dondo and Snowball looked on as they went out of sight.

The Lady asked "have they gone Dondo? He answered with a waggle of his tail and a twitch of his wonky ear, "yes", he said in his own way. He looked at Snowball and suggested they made for bed time as it was the end of another good day.

Dondo was very proud of Snowball and happy they had done well and were heroes again.

Snowball walked next to his best friend as they made their way towards the cottage, he was very happy to be in Leafy Lane Cottage with the best most magnificent friend in the world.

Because as we all now know he is

"Dondo the Magnificent."

The Wonderful Adventures of

Dondo the Magnificent

Story Four

SWALLOWS AND AFRICA.

Dondo was sleeping one day in the garden, he had rolled onto his back and between his snoozes and day dreaming about nothing in particular. Dondo looked across the wheat field close by, as he did in the distance he could hear the skylarks chirping away up high shouting about her secret nests that they were protecting, warning those below to keep their heads down and stay out of sight. He could hear the wood pigeons cooing and fluttering about in the big larch tree and occasionally he could hear the old owl in the evenings calling hoots from the big old oak tree.

Dondo also noticed some bigger white birds flying past and low their wings made a funny sound like creaky doors on an old barn as they took to the air from the pond at the end of the lane.

These were Swans, Dondo remembered them as had met them before when the Lady of the cottage took some biscuits to feed too them by the pond, Dondo often thought that that was a waste of good biscuit and should have been his biscuits.

Later in the afternoon be noticed some other birds flying low and soaring up high again, Dondo had thought that they were very fast flyers, they swooped down low and fast across the tops of the ears of wheat; whoosh. They were only small compared to the white Swans and Dondo had seen them before and was one of his favourite things to watch. He often day dreamed about being able to fly, he always wanted to know what it would be like to be able to move so quickly and with such ease.

The Lady in the cottage was cooking dinner, it was a Wednesday so cheese and vegetable flan was the dish of the day. Dondo's nose was already twitching as the lovely smell of the cooking in the kitchen wafted across the garden and went right up his nose and tickled his hungry alarm bell. Which we all know was right at the top of Dondo's nose right next to his biscuit button.

Snowball was lying next to Dondo, his nose had started to tickle too. Dondo looked across at him as he started to wake up from his deep sleep.

Earlier that day they had been for a long walk down to the post box so the Lady could send a letter to her son who lived far away.

So that afternoon after their walk, both Dondo and Snowball had found it very hard to stay awake when they returned from the walk. Within a few minutes of returning to the hollow under the apple tree their little eyelids just wouldn't stay open. Dondo thought Snowball looked funny with his twitchy nose and ears. Snowball opened one eye and in a moment said "What are you looking at Dondo?" his big friend replied with a "You!! Sleepy head! Did you catch a rabbit"?

"No I didn't" Snowball said, "they are always too fast and sneaky especially the biscuit flavoured one" "I know "said Dondo, I have chased him for years and still didn't get him but, "Maybe one day".

"What have you been doing"? Snowball asked as he stretched and gave a big slow yawn.

"I watched those birds flying across the fields, they are so fast, and they went zooming over the hedges then across the field top again" "Watching them has made me very hungry" Dondo reported.

Right at that minute the kitchen door opened and the Lady called "boys, dinner time" like two coiled springs both dogs shot off across the lawn galloping towards the cottage.

"Now, now, boys calm down and take your time". Said the Lady who had obviously realised the two dogs were hungry after the long walk earlier in the afternoon.

The two dogs were savouring the lovely Wednesday dinner of cheesy flan and vegetables with a little dash of homemade gravy and a few doggie biscuits for good measure, with the radio playing in the background - when all of a sudden there was

a big bump on the window, immediate
Snowball started barking and jumping
around, the Lady said in a shocked voice
"That's not normal" She put her knife and
fork down on the table "Let's go and have a
look Dondo". "That sounded like a football
bouncing off the glass!"

Dondo turned towards to door giving
Snowball a stare as he was still jumping
around barking Dondo and the Lady and went
to look and investigate, "Shush Snowball stop
making such a racket" Snowball was quite
startled and alarmed by the sound .

Dondo pushed open the kitchen door and had
a good look around but couldn't see anything,
the Lady followed him out, "what on earth
could that of been?" the Lady looked
quizzically. They looked around the garden

they looked around the spot where Snowball and Dondo had been sleeping all afternoon.

There were no big footballs, no white golf balls and no red cricket balls either, which could have been possible as there was a football pitch over the next field, down the lane was the golf club and across the park was the cricket club where the Lady often helped out on a Sunday afternoon making pies and sandwiches and of course her famous biscuits for the cricket teams.

Her friend PC Wobblebelly was an umpire there so she was always pleased to help out with the wife of the captain.

Scratching her head she said "oh come on Dondo, it was something or nothing let's get our dinner before it gets cold".

As they turned to return to the kitchen Dondo spotted something next to the table by the door, it was bird fluttering about on its side under the table, and it was looking dazed and a little confused.

Dondo stopped and pointed with his nose, the Lady said "Is there something there Dondo"? As she bent down to look the bird made a little "peep" noise, "oh my oh my poor thing "said the Lady, "you wait here Dondo", Dondo kept watching the little bird as it was clearly in some sort of distress.

The Lady rushed into the kitchen and came back with a soft tea towel, she bent down and scooped up the little bird very gently and made the bird settle before taking it into the kitchen. Dondo followed closely behind, the bird was quiet clearly alive but looked as far as she could tell a little bit dazed.

The Lady took it to the table by the window where there was some better light.

She put on her reading glasses and looked over the little bird carefully stretching out its wings one at a time while Dondo and Snowball looked on. The Lady checked its tail feathers and said nothing seems to be missing" he has tiny little legs and they seem ok. He has got one eye closed and the other open.

"I can't see if this little beauty has broken anything Boys", the Lady said." I'll give the vet a call after dinner and see if he can tell us what to do".

Dondo heard that" V" word, he didn't like the Vet and looked at the Lady with big saucer eyes and gulped…Snowball nearly choked on his mouthful of food and looked desperately at Dondo, oh no the V .. Vet! Oh no! Thought Snowball looking very worried. "No not for you softy pair" said the Lady to Dondo, "we'll see if we can with the help of

John the vet let this little one get airborne again".

After Dinner the Lady was using the tephalone and speaking to Vet John, she explained what had happened and told him when and where she and Dondo had found the little creature.

John the vet was on his way to the golf club and would call in he would be there in a few minutes.

After a short while a car drew up outside the garden gate and John the vet got out of the car and came in to the garden, the Lady went out to greet him "Hi John"" she called, Come on boys let's"" make John welcome, "no way" thought Dondo, Dondo hid under the table and Snowball hid behind Dondo.

John came in sat down and said "where are the dogs?" The Lady said " I don't know they were here a minute ago", she smiled at the vet and silently pointed under the table, "Oh there you are boys come on out I won't hurt you, Come on come on" he said to both dogs.

Dondo reluctantly and slowly came from under the table, Snowball very close behind, they both had a good fuss from John the vet and were soon at ease with him again. "That's better" John said, "so where is this little one?", "over here" said the Lady, "I've wrapped him up in a tea towel to keep him quiet and settled".

"That's good" said John as he undid the towel to reveal the little injured bird, "Oh a Swallow" Said John, that's unusual for a swallow to crash into a window"," hmmm" he said examining the wings one by one very gently extending the slim streamlined wings and passing a finger along each edge, "nothing broken here im pretty sure" he said.

He checked the tail feathers and checked his breathing, "Hmmm I think this little fellow has banged into the window at some speed and knocked himself out, little wonder he looks dazed and shaken up."

The vet turned and pick up his bag "I'll give him a little shot of medicine just in case and I would suggest you keep him quiet and settled, I'm sure that in the morning he will feel a bit brighter and be able to fly away happily."

The vet continued, "Let's hope so because it's getting late this September, they usually start to fly off to Africa at this time of year and if we don't get him fit and well he might miss the chance and if he leaves too late he could hit bad weather on the way down to Africa and we don't want that for him do we boys?" the vet looking own at the two dogs listening intently from under the table.

"Is it far for him to fly? Asked the Lady, "Oh yes" said john it takes about 4 to 6 weeks of hard flying and sleeping on the wing, all the way to South Africa, they travel through western France, across the Pyrenees, down eastern Spain into Morocco and across the Sahara. Have a look at a map it's amazing what they do".

"They don't usually land either and will stay in the air for as long as possible covering up to 200 miles a day. He will fly at low altitudes and find food on the way.

Despite putting some fat reserves before crossing large areas such as the Sahara Desert, they are vulnerable to starvation during these crossings. Migration is a hazardous time and many birds die from starvation, exhaustion and in storms, so it is very important we get him fit and airborne very soon."

"That's remarkable isn't it boys" said the Lady, "well we will look after him this evening and make sure he rests up for a while". "What shall I feed him?" Asked the Lady, The vet said nothing for the time being, the vet pointed to a tree branch outside where a bird feeder had fat and seeds mixed together hanging from a branch "that will be ok but only a tiny bit on a cocktail stick.

I suspect he will be ok, when he gets into the air he will find plenty of things to eat." - "Don't worry too much they are hardy things and quiet surprising".

The vet stood up and handed the little bird in the tea towel back to the Lady, he said "call me tomorrow evening if he hasn't taken off and ill call-in again."

"Thank you boys" John the vet said as he fussed them again," I hope to see you soon"

Dondo Looked at Snowball again and gulped! "Oh no you won't" Snowball whispered under his breath.

"I will "Said the Lady", "Thank you so much for coming by."

John the vet made his way to his car and drove off in the direction of the Golf Club. The Lady placed the little bird into a nest made from a pillow and an old bath towel and the tea towel she had already been using.

She took the little bird outside and rested him on the garden table which was under the veranda so he would be quite dry if it rained but there was none forecast so he should be safe and sound recovering outside and besides it was a warm day and afternoon too.

Dondo had finished his dinner and wandered outside to look at the bundle on the garden table, he wondered if the little bird would be ok, he certainly hoped so,

Snowball came to look too, the bird was quiet and silent no noises came from the makeshift nest. Dondo thought he injured bird must be sleeping,

So he settled down next to the table just to keep an eye on the visitor.

Snowball tip toed in quietly and gingerly settled next to Dondo to keep an eye on things too.

After a while and with fully bellies the two friends dropped off to sleep for a little snooze, Dondo awoke with a bit of a start! He became aware that something else was sitting on the garden table. It was Osmond the owl from the oak tree in Leafy Lane, Dondo jumped back, Snowball rolled off the decking with a tumble, and landed upside down on his head. Dondo knew Osmond as they often chatted across the road, Osmond would hoot and toot and Dondo would bark back.

Osmond lived in the Oak trees opposite the Lady's garden, he said ""Oh sorry Dondo I didn't mean to wake you up.

I just popped over to see how Stanley was getting on, Stanley? Said Osmond "who on earth is Stanley?" Dondo enquired in surprised disbelief! "Stanley, Stanley Swallow" said Osmond he is here isn't he? he had a bad crash on final approach this afternoon, we all thought he had copped it and that was the end of Stanley, but it looks like he's still with us, thank goodness and thanks to you and your Lady owner, good work there Dondo Osmond raised an eyebrow, the vet as well, very impressive indeed."

"So how do you know Stanley Swallow?" asked Dondo, "ahaha said Osmond flapping one wing like he was scratching an Itch, "he's

the fastest Swallow in the area Dondo",
"mmm yes a world record holder over three
wheat fields and the orchard at full speed,
didn't you know?"

"No" Said Dondo," I have been watching him
and his mates flying in the last few days",
"Yes" Osmond replied "they have been doing
training flights for the big trip the day after
tomorrow, they have a winter retreat in South
Africa you know? "

"Yes I had heard" grumped Dondo, wishing
he could have a warm winter retreat and
spend the whole year under apple trees. "So
what is his top speed?" Asked Dondo, "Well
the last time we checked about 8 or 9 fields
per minute", "Wow said Dondo that is fast."

Just then a little "Peep" came from the makeshift nest on the table, all of the onlookers stopped talking and looked into the tea towel, "hello Stanley its Osmond the Owl said how are you feeling old boy? "The little bird replied very quietly "Oooh my head hurts" said Stanley the Swallow. "What happened" "?

I was just coming in for a turn above the cottage then it all blacked out". "Yes Said Osmond Owl it looked like you came in too low old boy and missed the roof top you may have thought the window was a clear run through and bump! It stopped you in your tracks old friend".

"Oooh My head hurts he repeated". Take it easy" said Dondo "will get Lady"

Dondo set off into the house soon after the Lady came out after being tugged at by Dondo on her apron, "oooh I see she said hello little one".

Stanley turned to Osmond and said "who is this?" Osmond said "it's the Lady who lives here she is looking after you."

The Lady from a glass of water put a tiny drop of water on her smallest fingertip, she offered it close to the little birds beak, he lapped it off her fingertip she did it again and he drank some more, this made Stanley feel a little better but his head still hurt and his wing felt bruised.

The Lady wrapped him into the tea towel and told Osmond to leave and for Dondo and Snowball to leave alone and come back later in the morning. All three set off and could tell the Lady knew best.

In the morning the two dogs woke up and went straight out to see if Stanley was still there, Dondo jumped up to see, no he wasn't,

Dondo thought that Stanley had recovered and made his way during the night. that he hoped was a good thing. Snowball burst through the kitchen door out into the garden, "He's gone" said Dondo, Snowball looked confused, he replied "well he hasn't gone far Dondo! Look!"

Snowball pointed with his nose to the lawn, there in the middle of the lawn was Stanley, laid out flat nose down and wings spread out, Oh No thought Dondo, the two Dogs made their way across the grass and found Stanley face down in the green wet dew covered grass, "oh no Stanley" called Dondo, Stanley was cold and wet he had tried to take off early in the morning, he was still quite unwell and weak after his crash into the window the day before.

Stanley was weary and needed to get off the wet grass, Dondo picked him up using his mouth, and mindful that he had to be very gentle, he took Stanley to the cottage and gently put him on a chair near the garden table.

"Go get the Lady" Dondo instructed Snowball, Snowball ran quickly and barked at the Lady to come out and help. She knew immediately what Snowball barky shouting was at and followed him outside to see Dondo looking very worried.

"Oh no what has happened here then" said the Lady as she saw a wet and cold Stanley Sparrow, oh "silly boy Stanley" she said quietly to Him "you just couldn't wait ", She went inside and got another tea towel which had been warming on the kitchen stove, she came back and wrapped Stanley up and took him inside, she warmed him up next to the Kitchen cooker, she gave him sips of freshly made tea and some crumbs of her best biscuits, after half an hour or so Stanley perked up an bit and started to feel better.

The Lady said "Poor Stanley you must rest up, before your flight tomorrow, please take some time to rest or you will not be able to make your trip". Dondo looked on, Snowball was there too, both dogs looked so sorry for Stanley.

Osmond had heard some of the commotion and fluttered across into the cottage garden, he hooted at Dondo to come out, Dondo said "it's not good Ossy, he was in care with the Lady," I Think he tried to take off too soon and has run himself down, and he is cold and wet and so exhausted".

"Yes" said Osmond "he took a big bash yesterday let's hope he can recover before tomorrow, I will check in later". Osmond flew off back to his tree, Dondo returned to the kitchen, the Lady was busy Stanley was "peeping and chirping" which to Dondo was a good sign.

The Lady said Dondo and Snowball should go outside and leave the little Swallow rest and warm up.

Dondo and Snowball knew the Lady would do her best to look after Stanley and waited by the door for news of his recovery.

Later that morning the Lady appeared and Informed Dondo that Stanley was feeling much better, she suggested they make room for him on top of the garden table and let Stanley have some fresh air, let Stanley do his own thing and do it slowly and carefully. Let him have a go when he was quiet ready.

The Lady appeared with Stanley wrapped up in the tea towel she gently put him on the garden table top once more and whispered to the little bird not to take it too fast," just take your time". Stanley was very thankful and peeped "Cheers Lady".

Osmond had fluttered back across and asked for Dondo's update, "how is it all going old chap?" said Osmond, "he's resting still but he seems keen to get in the air again" replied Dondo.

Stanley called Osmond over, Osmond flew across the garden to the table, "what is it old chap", "Osmond I need to set off tomorrow but my wings are so stiff, and what can I do?" "Don't worry Stanley I'll have a bit of a chat with Dondo" said Osmond. Osmond waddled off to find Dondo and Snowball who were settled in the hollow under the apple tree.

Osmond said "we need a plan to get Stanley into the air, as his wings were stiff but other than his being tired all systems were working well and he was sure that once Stanley was airborne again he would soon get back into flying". The three of them sat silent looking at each other for a few minutes.

Dondo thought for a short while and then said quietly," I think I have an idea" the three stood chatting for a while deep in conversation, then Dondo all of a sudden ran across the garden from one end to the other.

Osmond was scratching his chin with his wing tip, he said to Dondo " yes, I think you have something there let's give the news to Stanley".

Stanley was feeling a little better when the three friends came over, Dondo and Snowball looked on as Osmond was whispering to Stanley, as they explained the plan Stanley's eyes lit up and he said "great idea guys" and he was ready to give the plan a go!

Snowball and Osmond went over to the lawn, Dondo picked up Stanley and took him over to the lawn, and carefully Stanley hopped off the tea towel. Snowball stood next to Dondo side by side, then Stanley hopped onto Snowball's back, Stanley took a few breaths,

Osmond said "are you alright old chap? "Yes fine replied Stanley Just a little bit stiff" Stanley then took another big hop onto Dondo's back Dondo moved side to side to keep Stanley balanced.

Osmond said to Stanley "move forward now and take hold of Dondo's dog collar", Stanley hopped through Dondo's thick fur and found the Blue leather dog collar. He took hold of it and held on tight.

Stanley looked up and forwards to see Osmond and Snowball both looking concerned but excited to see the little bird balanced on Dondo's tall back.

"Now remember what I said" Osmond instructing to Stanley "just for this first part hold your wings out let the air flow across them", "Ok" said Stanley slightly nervously he extended his stiff wings, "Im ready" Stanley called.

"Ok a few slow passes at first" said Osmond, "Off you go Dondo", Dondo started to walk up the garden, he stopped and turned at the top of the garden, he had a clear view and a clear run down the path with the breeze behind them.

Osmond held his wing up high then Snowball counted down in little barks 5-4-3-2-1 Go! Osmond dropped his wing to signal to Dondo to make his first run. "Go, go, go" Osmond shouted!

Dondo started to make his way down the garden, slowly at first, Stanley was holding on really tight his wings were held out straight, Dondo was trying not to go too fast on the first run, Stanley's wings were working well and the breeze was a welcome feeling to Stanley, it was good to feel the cool wind under his wings once again.

As they reached the end of the garden they stopped and Dondo made a turn so they were facing up the garden path. Dondo asked "are you ok up there Stanley?"

Stanley said "yes all good that was good", "im ready for the next pass" "great ok hold on" Dondo shouted.

Osmond shouted over to Dondo "a little faster this time Dondo you're into wind", "Ok" said Dondo, "will do " Snowball counted down in barky language again 5-4-3-2-1 Go! Osmond dropped his wing and Dondo galloped full speed down the garden, this time the breeze was in Stanley face and his wings began to flutter, the air was lifting the feathers on his wings and tail feathers, Dondo stopped near the garden gate and only just as he was running out of garden. "Phew that was close Dondo" said Stanley.

Osmond came over and said "that was great Stanley are you OK to try again", "Oh Yes" Stanley said "Dondo is really fast" Dondo was panting a little, So Snowball suggested they have a little rest and a drink, then try again. Dondo and Stanley Stood with Osmond and Snowball, discussing the next steps in Dondo's plan for a few minutes in a huddle on the lawn.

The Lady of the cottage was looking out of the kitchen window she saw what they were doing whispered to herself, "What are these four up to?"

Dondo made his way to the bottom of the garden again, Stanley now feeling much better and stronger was ready, Osmond held his wing up, Snowball counted down in his barks, 5-4-3-2-1 Go!

Again Stanley held on as the mighty Dondo took off at full speed faster and faster Dondo went, the wind was really lifting and fluttering all the feathers in Stanley's wings, woohoo!! Shouted Stanley as Dondo started to slow a little late and came to a sharp stop again sliding on the grassy path as he was running out of garden.

Dondo was getting hot and was panting, Osmond came over to check Stanley was ready for the most important part of the plan, they talked nodding in agreement as Osmond was explaining to Stanley how the next run was going to go and what he should do when he heard the signal.

"I will give the signal and you do the next part Stanley" said Osmond, "ok" replied Stanley "What is the signal going to be?" "Release!" Osmond instructed." Its release" They all nodded in agreement that this was the time for the final run.

Osmond and Snowball retreated to the edge of the hollow near the apple tree, Osmond slowly raised his wing, Dondo looked down the garden pointing his nose directly at the garden gate, Snowballs heart was racing, Stanley took a deep breath, and the Lady of the cottage came out and stood watching with her arms folded.

Dondo lowered his head a little ready for the start signal, Snowball looked at Osmond and Osmond nodded for Snowball to start the count down 5-4-3……."stop, stop ! Stanley shouted", "What is it?" Dondo asked, Osmond and Snowball made their way over very concerned something serious had or was going to happen.

Stanley said "to my new dear friends, I would just like to thank you all for your help and care Thank you very much. I'll never forget this day."

"You are welcome old chap" said Osmond, "Yes said Dondo you are always welcome,

come back and see us again one day", "I will" said Stanley, "Right im ready chaps let's go!".

The four took up their positions again Snowball and Osmond were near the apple tree, Dondo and Stanley were backed up as far in the garden as they could to get the longest run down the garden.

Dondo lowered his nose once more , Stanley held on, wings extended, Osmond held his wing up high, Osmond nodded to Snowball, Snowball slowly counted 5-4-3-2-1 GO ! Osmond dropped his wing to signal to Dondo to Go!

Dondo took off this time, fast, very fast, Stanley was holding on, the wind this time was fierce in their faces Stanley's wings began to lift and flutter, Dondo continued to accelerate as the pair passed the garden table and then the apple tree zooming past Snowball and Osmond.

Osmond waited a second then shouted at the top of his hoot "REALEASE" Stanley immediately let go of Dondo's blue leather collar as the wind rushed at his face and under his body he raised his tail feathers a little as his wings filled with air and Whoosh, Stanley was airborne!

He shot over the garden gate and straight up over the road way of leafy lane and up and up high into the sky.

He flew over the wheat fields and circled back towards the cottage, Dondo had come to a crash sliding into the garden gate with a bump, he stood up to watch as Stanley soared higher and higher his wings working again, from below he could hear Dondo Snowball and Osmond....and the "Lady" cheering as he somersaulted and turned loop the loop and barrel rolled in a very happy and joyful aerial display.

Stanley turned tight and fast over the golf course and across the cricket ground, it felt great to be flying again he was really enjoying the flight he realised that he was again, strong and well.

He flew in a low pass across the wheat fields he could see the cottage ahead and below and the friends waving him farewell and a safe journey to his Sunny South Africa.

Bye Stanley shouted, thanks for everything. Whoosh he flew fast and very low past Dondo ruffling his fur and wobbling Dondo's wonky ear as he passed at high speed through and across the garden then up up high and away.

Dondo turned to see the Lady coming across the lawn, she stroked him fondly on the head, well done Dondo you are a clever dog.

Osmond came over to see Dondo who was still panting after his runs up and down the garden," Well Done Dondo great work and a great plan" Congratulated Osmond, "Thank you for all your help too" Dondo replied, Snowball came over too "Great work Dondo" said a proud Snowball, "great work to you too mate you are a great count downer" said Dondo, as they turned toward the cottage.

Osmond flew off and returned to his home in the oak tree in Leafy Lane.

Dondo and Snowball returned to the hollow and chatted and laughed about Stanley and the whooshes and zooms he had done overhead in the sky.

To greet them both was a biscuit from the proud Lady she had cooked freshly that morning.

This made Dondo think that this was the best place in the world to spend time with his best friend Snowball and the wonderful friends he had made out in leafy lane.

This did make him feel magnificent and he was proud to be known as Dondo the Magnificent.

The Wonderful Adventures of

Dondo the Magnificent

Story Five

Summers End Adventure.

The long warm Summer was coming to it end , the days were moving towards the end of September, the days became cooler and the days shorter, the flowers and plants some of the trees began to lose their vibrant green colour, golden ambers and browns started to emerge in the tree tops.

Some of the birds have moved on so birdsong in the mornings at dawn wasn't the same gloriously chorused welcome to the new day as it was in the previous spring, there was a change in the weather. The Lady and PC Wobblebelly would often say as the 1st of September passed there is a bite in the air.

Dondo and Snowball had taken to snoozing and day dreaming between meals and long walks on the veranda, it was partially under cover and although the beds they had to rest in were comfortable they were no match for the hollow under their favourite apple tree half was down the garden.

Occasionally Snowball and Dondo would waddle down their slowly and flop into the hollow, somehow it felt a little strange, not so familiar, perhaps because it was now colder and wetter with almost daily rain showers, the hollow was not as welcoming as it was in high summer when it was cool and snoozily soft and comfortable.

The space under the apple tree was starting to become full of apples dropped off the tree by the rainstorm wind and rain

The Lady of the cottage in Leafy Lane would come daily and collect the Windfalls take them back to the kitchen wash them and prepare them for an apple pie or her famous crumbles and tartlets. It was a good year for apples, just enough rain and lots of sunshine would assure a sweeter apple.

Out the back of the Garden the Lady had a small vegetable patch where she grew cabbage and potatoes, beetroots, rhubarb and salad leaves, her tomatoes were raised in old plant pots given to her many years ago by her grandfather these were under the veranda where the sunshine was generous and the cover was good, she always had a good crop.

She never knew the variety of the tomatoes as she always grew them from seed, each last day of February planting them out at the end of March from the little rickety old green house, potting them up at the end of April, the name of the variety may had been forgotten, what was remembered was they were sweet and vibrant red, with that smell and taste of a home grown tomatoes.

The Lady shouted to Dondo and Snowball to come and get their walking leads on as it was time to go to the village to get some food, Dondo went to the kitchen door followed someway behind by Snowball, Snowball didn't want to go to the village and he wasn't keen today.

It was a long walk for nothing as far as he was concerned, he always though he had the worse deal as his legs were little and to keep up with the Lady and Dondo who had much longer legs, he had to march twice as fast.

Twice as fast meant twice the hard work, twice the energy and it felt like twice as far, but he only gets one biscuit the same as Dondo, so especially as he didn't feel like a walk, he didn't think it was right that the village was the same distance away for Dondo as it was for him.

Dondo had his bright blue leather lead put on with no fuss, he always loved his walk and was more than pleased to sit patiently as the Lady whispered kind words to him as his soft lead was clicked on to his collar, Snowball today wasn't so pleased to have his lead on, he bowed his head and put his paws down, he wouldn't sit still.

Snowball ran off and hid in the flower border, "A ha" said the Lady smiling, "some mischief has come to play today". "Come on Snowball" the Lady called, "it's time to go", Snowball continued to hide, he ran from one side of the house to the other.

"Oh dear Dondo, the butchers will be closing soon" Said the Lady, "if we don't get a move on, can you have a talk with your friend Snowball please, tell him sausages will sell out soon if we don't get there and the butcher will not be pleased if we are late to collect my order and that means you won't get your"….treat.

Before the Lady could finished her words Dondo was off chasing Snowball round the garden with his blue lead trailing behind "come on Snowy, what's up with you?" Dondo barked at Snowball, not wanting Snowballs bad mood to be risking Dondo's treat from Ben at the butchers shop

"I don't want to walk all that way" he replied. "Well if you want sausages for dinner you had better get your lead on and quick about it Dondo barked his instruction a little louder, "Don't forget if we are going to the butchers we get a little treat from Ben the butcher" Dondo said as he was trying to coax Snowball into making and effort to hurry up.

The Lady called to Snowball holding his lead out stretched in her hand, "come on little one", she gestured for him to go over, and he walked over as if it was a real uphill effort. In his mind he was saying do I really have to?

The Lady bent down and clipped Snowballs lead on, she looked him right in the eye and said come on Snowball cheer up and ruffled his furry head.

Reluctantly Snowball joined Dondo and the Lady as they made their way through the garden gate out onto Leafy Lane. The lane was now starting to show that cooler days, much cooler days were a head. Some leaves had started to be shed from the tall tree that encircled the cricket ground

Cooler days were definitely here, as they turned in to the buttercup field, there were not many buttercups in flower now and a cool breeze greeted them as they joined the track through the field, "Im pleased I put my coat on" said the Lady to Dondo, its quiet nippy through here boys. The Lady marched ahead and the dogs were left to run free through the field and stop at the top gate.

The Lady soon caught them up and clicked their leads together as they walked the last few yards in to the Village, the Lady stopped at the post box and posted several letters, then she went to the card shop to buy some birthday cards, her stock was running low she said and topped up with a few more for upcoming birthday celebrations.

Each time she went into a shop she clipped the dog leads to a ring outside the shops, all of the shops had them as there were a lot of dog owners in the Village and surrounding areas.

The boys sat patiently. As they did Dondo spotted the Butchers shop at the end of the Main Street.

There he could make out Ben serving customers in the butchers shop, Ben was listening to a customer then turned and bent right down in to the window display of fine meats and chickens, he took a bunch of sausages in his big hands.

As he did Ben glanced up and Spotted the Lady coming out of the card shop and the two dogs waiting for her, Ben smiled to himself and was looking forwards to seeing the boys and the Lady for a quick chat, the shop wasn't too busy and it was soon time to close to this would be a nice end to a day in the butchers shop.

The Lady crossed the road and made her way to the library where she handed in a couple of books she had read, she told the librarian that she would come another day to choose another one as she still had one at home unfinished which she was enjoying.

All the way down the street Dondo couldn't take his eyes of the door of the butchers shop, he desperately wanted to see Ben the Butcher, Ben was a tall man with broad shoulders and a friendly face, he was the captain of the cricket team so he and the Lady know each other quiet well.

The Lady came out of the Library and turned to go into the butchers shop, the boys were clipped to the ring outside, as she went in Ben said "Hello how are we today then"? "Oh hello ben how are things, yes we are fine just popped down to collect my order said the Lady clipping the dogs outside on the wall,

"I've got it all ready for you it's all there and I've put some extra beef in for the pasties for this Sundays match, are you still ok to make a few? Now then where are my tow favourite dogs?

Ben came from round the glass counter top filled with pies and all thing delicious, he reached to the top of the cabinet where he had on a piece of serving paper cut two slices of pork pie from the big pie in the display case.

Ben broke them up into smaller pieces, he called Dondo over first, Dondo stepped forward and sat down, the butcher offered him a bit of Pie and Dondo offered his paw and gently took it from Ben, Good Boy Dondo Said Ben.

Now for Snowball, Ben took a little bit of the pie and held it out, Snowball came up sniffed the pie and turned and went back to where he was sitting. "Oh dear said Ben I've upset Snowball the Lady tutted "tut tut Snowball" she said how can you refuse some of Bens homemade pork pie".

Dondo Said Can I have yours? Snowball said if you want it, turning his nose in the air.

Dondo heard Ben call him again, without wasting any time or second thought he stepped forward and held out his paw, Ben stooped down and Dondo gently took the piece of pie from Ben.

Ben stood up and said to the Lady, "Im Looking forward to our match on Sunday, it should be a good one and I think we have a good chance of winning this one". "So am I" said the Lady as she packed her order into her shopping bag, "we will, all three of us be there to help cheer you on".

That's great said Ben and I hope Snowball has got his appetite back. Snowball looked up with a sad face when he heard his name, oh come on Snowball said Ben cheer up, it will be a good day, you and Dondo can wallow under the trees and im sure you will get a sandwich or a sausage roll or two.

Dondo was pleased with the forecast and he was definitely looking forward to a gentle day listening to the cricket match with a full belly of sandwiches and sausage rolls. The Lady looked at Dondo, she knew exactly what he was thinking.

Ben said I'll see you Sunday then? "Yes you will Ben thanks for my order and thanks for everything" the Lady made her way out of the shop and walked down the Main Street Dondo by her side and Snowball trailing behind in a sulk.

Dondo lead the way as they turned in to Leafy Lane, the gate at the buttercup field was open, the Lady and Snowball stepped thought as she turned she closed the gate and checked no one else was in the field before letting the dogs off their leads, she let Dondo's lead free and then Snowballs.

Dondo shot off down the track and skipped and jumped as he went, Snowball sat down, and he just sat there. The Lady has walked several yards on before she noticed that Snowball wasn't trying to keep up with Dondo as usual, She turned and saw the little fellow on his own, "Come on Snowball" she said Little Snowball just started walking the was no running in him today.

The Lady made a mindful note to herself to keep an eye on Snowball, this was not his usual mood and she was slightly concerned about him being so unhappy.

They wandered through the buttercup field and when they arrived at the bottom gate Dondo was waiting for them, He too was thinking as why Snowball was so grumpy.

They made their way down the lane and towards the cottage, as they got closer Dondo heard the squeak of a police issue bicycle coming down the lane, "oh no" Dondo thought "not Mr Wobbleybelly".

Yes It was PC Wobblebelly on his way to the cricket club, he slowed down and got off his Bicycle, "Heeello you three" he greeted the Lady and the two dogs, "how are we all?"

Oh we are ok thanks Bill, said the Lady, we have just been into see Ben to pick up our order, How are you Bill?

The Policemen was walking with his bike, by her side I am very well thank you, im calling in on the cricket club to check the pitch and make sure the clubhouse is ready for our big match on Sunday, Yes im looking forward to it said the Lady.

So am I and it's not just because the best pies and sandwiches will be on offer, it's always a great day out to come to the last cricket match of the year. See you Sunday PC Wobblebelly Said as he crossed the lane and into the gate of the cricket club.

Snowball held back when PC Wobblebelly crossed the road, the Lady spotted his little nervousness, Snowball continued walking behind Dondo, "mmm" the Lady Thought" for some reason little one isn't very happy". When they got back to the cottage the Lady picked up Snowball and had a good fuss.

He seemed ok she thought he just wasn't his normal happy little doggy self, "Don't be sad Snowball "said the Lady she tickled him under the chin and placed him down, "go see Dondo see if he can cheer you up" she went into the cottage to start on the dinner.

Dondo had settled into the hollow under the apple tree, Snowball slowly walked over to him, Dondo looked at Snowball and said "what is wrong little Snowball, Snowball slumped down a little way from Dondo. Looking very sad.

"Come on tell me I could help pleaded Dondo, come on Snowball the Lady is worried about you".

Well said Snowball" it's the clicket match "the clicket match?" replied Dondo, "do you mean the Cricket match"? "!"Yeah said Snowball "it's over there isn't it?", "well, yes" said Dondo "that's where they play cricket in that big field with the men in white jumpers and the tea and sandwiches It's the nice peaceful time."

It's a really nice day Snowball, what's not to like,"?

Snowball had a tears in his eyes, "well Dondo that's where I was thrown out of the car, that's why I came to you for help I had been dropped off and abandoned there at the clicket place and never saw my owner again, so I don't want to go back the Lady might do the same".

Dondo was speechless, "oh no"! He thought he was so sorry that Little Snowball thought he would be thrown back out on his own, and that the cricket club held such a bad memory for Snowy.

Dondo put his paw on Snowballs shoulder, "you silly little dog said Dondo, the Lady wouldn't throw you out, and I wouldn't let her, you are so loved Snowball, try not and think of the past. We are family and We are a team, the best doggy detectives in the Village.

Dondo consoled little Snowball for a few minutes before the Lady called Dinner boys from the Kitchen door, Dondo looked at Snowball , Snowball looked at Dondo, Come on said Dondo its Sausages!!! Both dogs walked side by side across the garden towards the house, the smell of Ben the butchers

Sausages filled their little noses as did the lovely gravy they both loved.

The weekend was a few days where the Lady did chores in the garden, she collected her potatoes and lettuce for the Sunday banquet at the Cricket club, Snowball was feeling a little more spritely and followed the Lady round her garden almost as if he was watching and learning, Dondo was less interesting in gardening, he was more interested in wallowing in the hollow, under his apple tree.

Before they knew it Sunday had arrived the Leafy Lane was busy with cars arriving for the end of season cricket match.

It was a warm Sunny September Sunday, the air was full of the start of autumn, but still warm enough for a wonderful day of cricket.

The Lady had been hard at work since the early hours making pies and sandwiches for the cricket team's half time tea lunch.

PC Wobblebelly arrived and took two huge boxes of fruit pies and another tray of sandwiches Fingers off warned the Lady to PC Wobblebelly I've counted them all " Oh Ok" said PC Wobblebelly looking sheepish.

The cricket match started at 10 o'clock and the first "tock" of the day sounded out as the hard cricket ball hit the wood of the cricket bat,

Dondo had walked across Leafy Lane into the Cricket club with the Lady and Snowball, Snowy was a little apprehensive at first but Dondo are assured him all was ok they both sat beside the Lady who in turn sat on her favourite bench under the old oak tree to watch Ben the Butcher, PC Wobblebelly and John the Vet play cricket.

Stay here boys the Lady said , she went in to the Cricket Pavilion, which was very old , dusty and somewhat rickety, she was helping other ladies make the tea and sandwiches , See, Dondo said to Snowball what could be better.

Snowball didn't reply, but as Dondo laid back and wriggled his back into the cool grass under the shade of the big chestnut tree, he lay there peacefully although he could hear laughing and men shouting, then he heard the Lady shouting "oh no come here oh no!"

Dondo glanced around to see Snowball chasing the cricket ball, the players had stopped the game and were standing with hands on their hips shouting "Who's is this little dog" or "Dog on the pitch" "Stop the game" "Dog Interrupts Play" someone shouted from the small crowd watching from the club house and all because Snowball was running round and round chasing and trying to steal the ball, "What is he doing now barked Dondo?" Dondo ran onto the pitch to catch Snowball.

Snowball saw Dondo coming on to the cricket pitch and started to run faster with the ball, turning on a sixpence in the other direction so quickly and fast.

Snowball was beginning to think he was good at cricket as no one could catch him, after all if both cricket teams couldn't be bothered to chase him then Dondo, the Lady, PC Wobblebelly, Ben the butcher and some, in fact most of the opposing team chasing him was the next best thing, he thought this was great and was the best fun he had had in ages.

Dondo slipped past PC Wobblebelly like a bullet, PC Wobblebelly was seriously angry and now was starting to march sternly towards Snowball with a very terse look on his face Snowball was zig zagging in and out of the cricketer's legs.

Dondo was shouting in barky language "Snowball stop this is not a game for you or us" Snowball took no notice he was running so fast his ears were flapping so he couldn't hear the desperate calls from Dondo "Seriously Snowball drop the ball and come and sit down or you will be in big trouble".

Snowball continued, He zoomed past PC Wobblebelly through his legs past the stumps and down towards the other end of the pitch. Cricket team members jumping to the left and right as they scrambled to stop the super-fast Snowball with the bright red cricket ball in his mouth.

The Lady Shouted across as she ran after Snowball to Dondo, "Donnnndo" she cried "Do something" "Pleeease"!

Dondo quickly thought of a plan he went over to the side of the cricket pitch, he stood up on his back legs, and shouted at the top of his voice in barky barking language directly at Snowball "Snowball! Snowball "Freeeeeesh Bissssscuits"!

Immediately and very calmly Snowballs one dog cricket game came to an end, Snowball stopped running, he calmly walked over to PC Wobblebelly, Snowball puffing and panting with his tongue hanging out dropped the ball quiet near PC Wobblebelly's and Ben the butchers feet both men were panting too following the chase, they looked at each other in disbelief.

Snowball trotted over to where Dondo was waiting under the big chestnut tree.

Snowball came and sat in front of Dondo, the Lady came over too and quickly put Dondo's lead onto Snowballs collar, The Lady retuned to the cricket Pitch and was apologising to each of the team members.

Ben took her gently by the arm, don't worry" he said it's not the first time play has been interrupted and im sure it won't be the last", PC Wobblebelly looked over and gave a reassuring wink and smile to the Lady "Its ok he whispered"

The cricketers soon got back into playing the game and cheers from the watching crowd were heard once again, shouts of LWB, Leg! , Umpire! Or Six! , the "Tock" sound of the ball on bat were soon relaxing sounds in the background making for a perfect Summer Sunday afternoon.

Snowball felt for some reason he was in trouble and to make him sure of that Dondo was giving him a hard time, Dondo was laying down on the grassy slope next to the cricket pitch his paws crossed and head rested on them. "So there are NO Sausage rolls Dondo? Snowball enquired again for the 10th time, "Nope not for you Snowball, you have been a naughty dog" "Oh come on" said Snowball "you cannot be serious, it's just a game" cried Snowball.

"No Not a Game you nearly stopped the last match of the season. What is worse you made the Lady upset" said Dondo"

"Not a good thing to do" Dondo barked looking straight into Snowballs eyes.

The morning rolled on and the cricket match came to a half way point, it was time for lunch and a break for a while, Sandwiches and lots of cups of tea were served from the Club house Pavilion.

PC Wobblebelly was at the front of the queue with a biggest plate of sandwiches, sausage rolls and muffins, "goodness me" said the Lady "are you sure you can eat all of that Bill"? She asked PC Wobblebelly, That's why they call him Wobblebelly said Bill the butcher laughing.

The Lady asked one of her friends to take over serving tea, she said I'll be back in a few minutes, she took a few ham sandwiches and a couple of sausage rolls on a paper plate and set off towards her dogs, Dondo Spotted her coming down the steps of the pavilion, Dondo sat up attentively as she approached. Here you go you two said the Lady, she placed the plate on the wooden bench.

I hope you are happy with yourself Snowball what a performance! She stood there hands on her hips looking disapproving of Snowballs outburst earlier with the cricket ball.

She said to the dogs not to eat the sandwiches until she returned in a few minutes. She was going to get her lunch before the start of the second half of the match. They were instructed not to touch the lunches as they would all sit together and eat their lunches when the second half of the match would get underway.

Dondo turned to Snowball and said I told you she would be mad with you, Snowball huddled down and hid his face, Dondo had settled down and was sitting again paws crossed and his chin on them watching the activity at the pavilion Snowball was very quiet and was feeling sorry and rather hungry.

When the Lady returned five minutes later she sat down with her cup of tea and sandwiches, she placed her plate on the bench, she settled just as the pavilion bell rang out as the players moved back onto the pitch signalling the start of the second half.

She was looking forward to the second half and always looked forward to this match it could become so exciting but, "What's this!" she said as she took the napkin off the dogs lunch, I don't believe this boys "she said sternly, who has had the sausage rolls? Dondo was it you? Dondo looked up at the half empty plate both his ears dropped, he looked so disappointed, the Lady turned to Snowball, I thought I told you boys not to eat the food, oh dear oh dear she scoffed as she sat down.

Dondo gruffed at Snowball whispering "What are you doing Snowball? "It wasn't me it was you!" replied Snowball, "im in enough trouble already why would I eat them?" "Because you are greedy", "no im not"!

Snowball gruffed back. The two boys argued in barky language and they were starting to get louder and louder and so loud it became too much for the Lady to tolerate!

The cricket players were beginning to be distracted too by all the racket and barking coming from Dondo and Snowball, The Lady stopped eating her sandwich she put down her lunch and cup of tea, she clearly had had enough and split the dogs up.

She put Dondo at one end of the bench and the noisy augmentative Snowball at the other. "Now be quiet you two shushsh!!" The Lady held her finger to her lips and gave a last "shush boys".

The boys knew they were in trouble and did settle down.

Dondo was getting hungry as was Snowball every now and then Snowball would let out a little gruff just under his breath Dondo would reply with a "yes it was"!! Gruff under his breath.

After being told to be quiet several times by the Lady, Dondo rolled onto his back and was looking at the sky, he eyes drifted across to the cover of the big chestnut tree they were sitting beneath.

As he gazed up Dondo spotted a big bushy grey tail high on a branch flicking back and forward right up in the tree top, sometimes it would flick to the right and sometimes to the left, most of the time it flicked up and down. Dondo thought it certainly was a happy tail.

As it flicked Dondo could see flakes of something falling gently from the top branches, as they made their way down they looked like small leaves falling from the tree, as he followed one on its journey down from the tree it landed on Dondo's nose.

Going a little cross eyed Dondo gently put his tongue out to taste the funny leaf, But It wasn't a leaf, it was tasty flaky pastry and just like the tasty pastry the Lady Made, in fact it was exactly the same as the Lady made when she made....SAUSAGE ROLLS!!

"Hold on" Dondo thought, "How did those crispy flakes of sausage roll pastry get up there and why were they up there?" Dondo whispered to Snowball, "Hey Snowy look up there", "where"? Said Snowball "straight up there", Dondo pointed one of his Paws "there up there he said quietly", Snowball could see something but it was hidden behind the big broad leaves of the chestnut tree.

Then from behind the big leaf was a face, a little cheeky face, with pointy ears and a tuft of white fur on the top of each ear. A twitchy nose and always scratching his belly.

Who is that Said Dondo? I don't know said Snowball just then a piece of sausage dropped right next to the Lady, she stopped watching the cricket game in front of her, she looked and checked that the two boys were at opposite end of the bench then slowly looked up.

"Oh my word" said the Lady look at that little devil, at that the cheeky faced squirrel looking very pleased with himself made himself known.

Dondo recognised him, it was a well know local one squirrel crime wave, he was well known for stealing the bird food from the Lady's bird table in the garden in leafy lane. The Lady and Dondo knew him well and knew him as ……….."Cecil the sneaky squirrel"

Hey losers! Shouted the Squirrel in a string of squeaks rubbing his ears as he did, he shouted down to Snowball and Dondo

"Lovely Snacks Dondo thanks for the food treat boooys, it was soooo tasty!"

"You got us into trouble Cecil and that's not a nice thing to do IS IT? Dondo barked back.

"No way! - So what doggy, my belly Is full up now "squeaked the Squirrel, as he rubbed his tummy round and round laughing at the two dogs below,

" do I look as if a care."! He laughed

Then Cecil hopped across to another tree branch and scampered down the trunk, he sped past Snowball laughing at Snowball as he ran. Loser! Cecil called out with a slimy grin on his face, he really was a bad piece of work thought Snowball.

Dondo barked "you are a robber Cecil I'll get you"

The Lady stood up, Cecil ran between her making her jump and topple over, the Lady screamed, Dondo went to run after Cecil, he was so angry Snowball had missed his lunch and he had had his stolen, and worst of all it was all down to sneaky Cecil.

Dondo's blue dog lead caught in the leg of the bench and as the Lady stood up the bench fell over backwards the sandwiches and tea falling over the tea cup smashed, the plate of cake and biscuits reduced to messy crumbs on the grassy bank. "Oh My, Oh My " said the Lady in a real panic.

PC Wobblebelly looked around to see the Lady and the dogs in a right tangle, Dog leads and Bench over on its side, Snowball stuck under the bench, Dondo was going mad at the Squirrel who had by now made his way across the cricket pitch and over the hedge into leafy Lane where it looked to Dondo as if he was making his way into their Garden.

PC Wobblebelly was on his way he came over and helped he Lady to her feet, Dondo was still pulling on the bench unaware that Snowball was stuck under it, PC Wobble belly released Dondo's lead and Dondo shot off across the cricket pitch and stopped the cricket match for a second time.

Dondo could see Cecil jumping from branch to branch and across the lane scampering up and down the trees and making great big jumps from branch to branch and tree to tree.

Dondo was following close behind, Cecil jumped down onto the big hedge in the Lady's garden ah ha Dondo thought " I knew it!", Cecil was going to make trouble on Dondo's turf.

The Lady and PC Wobblebelly were getting things straight again and had put the bench back to where it should be against the chestnut tree, PC Wobblebelly said "I'll get you some fresh tea, sit there and take a breath for a few minutes." Off he set and soon came back with a tray loaded with a tea pot and biscuits and some fresh sandwiches.

"You have not had a good afternoon really have you"? Said PC Wobblebelly "No I don't think I have Bill thank you for the tea". The Lady said have you seen the dogs? PC

Wobblebelly said no, oh no she said I hope they have gone running off.

Just then they both heard a muffled whimper, the Lady walked around the bench to find little Snowball scrunched up in his lead which had caught up in the bench legs, he was dangling from the bench one leg up and the other leg down, his head was stuck in the Lady's handbag.

The policeman soon freed him away and the Lady said to Snowball "you had better go and find Dondo", Snowball raised himself on his back legs and gave a roff raff bark that to the Lady sounded remarkably like OK!

The Lady said to PC Wobblebelly Im starting to hear things now. "No" said The Policeman "He said OK," they both looked at each other and laughed.

Snowball cautiously crossed the lane and arrived in the garden to find Dondo at the kitchen window, Cecil the squirrel has got into the kitchen and was running amok in the kitchen cupboards pots and pans were dropping and the noise was quiet disturbing.

The squirrel stopped on the kitchen sink knocking cups and a few saucers over as he came right up to the glass window, he pushed his nose against the glass, he looked directly at Dondo, with his paws on his little hips he said "so what are you going to do now Doggy?", Dondo growled a real deep growl like Snowball had never heard before "Im going to get you one day Cecil" "Oh yeah well your too slow I can out run you any day" Cecil laughed and mocked Dondo doing a little dance on the windowsill. Singing "Watchayougonnado dodo!! Watchayougonnado dodo!! Dondo Dumbo!"

Cecil jumped up to the top window and scampered out of the kitchen only just out of reach of Dondo. Dondo Snapped to try and catch him but he was too quick and very agile, to the right, to the left he jumped so fast, he jumped onto the garden table, he ran around and around the garden Dondo following and Snowball following Dondo.

Soon they were starting to feel a bit exhausted, after all they had no lunch, and Snowball was beginning to think how long we can keep this up! Dondo shouted to Snowball "we need a plan Snowy, we can't keep this up all afternoon!"" I know!" shouted Snowball.

Dondo said to Snowball "keep him running I'll be back in a few seconds I need to see someone", Dondo made a big leap over the fence whilst Snowball followed Cecil.

As Cecil teased Snowball by zig zagging down the garden and across the other side near the hedge then criss cross across the lawn up the apple tree and down again come on short legs run faster! "Snowball was barking furiously as he chased the little monster round the garden, and was getting very tired.

After a few minutes Dondo reappeared, "av ya been to see the coppers then have you Dondo doggy" "Gone to tell your tales then have we?" teased Cecil as he flashed by Dondo, Snowball was close behind.

Dondo walked to the end of the Garden near the garden table, Dondo didn't say a word but sat down facing the garden gate, Cecil wiggled himself in silly little dance sticking his tongue out and waving his ears in front of Dondo, singing "whatchagonnadodopey" Dondo just sat there staring directly at Cecil, Dondo signalled to Snowball to come and quietly sit beside him.

Cecil continued to make fun of the two dogs, Dondo just stared thinking how stupid Cecil was as Cecil continued his mockery.

Then, Snowball smiled, his eyes widened, he said "oh yes", Dondo smiled too he said "oh yes definitely oh yes!", just then the sky behind Cecil went very dark for a second or two, Cecil looked around to see why, as he did he was met by a almighty whoosh, and a Sharpe pair of claws caught hold of the squirrels shoulders and lifted him clean off the grass.

Yaaaaaooouch!! shouted Cecil as Osmond Owl had done a perfect silent dive and captured Cecil from the rear by surprise, Cecil didn't know what had hit him, as Osmond flapped his enormous wings he made a wide turn above the cottage "Leave this to me boys" Osmond called to the dogs below and flapped off into the direction of the cricket club.

Whoosh! They flew low past the Lady and PC Wobblebelly who were deep in conversation as the peculiar sight flew past them, they looked and looked at each other in disbelief and laughed, did you see what I just seen? Said PC Wobblebelly, "I think so" said the Lady.

Dondo and Snowball were barking with delight and chasing their tails as the little monster was being "relocated". The plan had worked perfectly so far.

Osmond flew high over the cricket club and across the golf club and over into the woods at the back of the village pond, over the fields and far away they flew Cecil's little legs dangling beneath him.

"I don't like heights" he protested "put me down"," I'll have you whoever you are!"

"I'll get you for this you pesky big fat bird" he shouted.

Osmond flew low down and in a sweeping turn low to the ground in a small filed next to a wood, he placed Cecil onto a log, "There you go Little Monster enjoy your new home."

"You Loser" shouted Cecil waving his clenched fist as the big graceful bird flew away high into the sky.

Osmond flapped his enormous wings and made a straight line towards the cottage, it only took a few minutes as he passed over the cricket club again. As he arrived in the garden Dondo and Snowball were waiting below,

The Lady and PC Wobblebelly walked into the garden just as Osmond landed, Oh Look said he Lady it's that Owl we saw a few minutes ago. "Yes no Squirrel this time" laughed PC Wobblebelly.

The Lady opened the kitchen door all was well, Dondo had managed to squeeze through the old dog flap in the back door and make his way into the cottage and has quickly tidied up the cups that had been disturbed by the evil Cecil Squirrel.

"Well what a day Boys" the Lady said, "I think you two need a treat of Sausages and A slice of Pork Pie for your supper", Dondo looked at Snowball he said "great work Snowy", "great work indeed" said Snowball "we are a great team eh?" "Yes we are the best" said Dondo.

Osmond made his goodbyes to the boys and had been pleased to help get rid of that nuisance of a squirrel, Dondo thanked him for his quick action and waved him off as he flew back to the old oak tree opposite the garden

As the shorter evening closed in Dondo and Snowball settled down after a very tasty Dinner, PC Wobblebelly made his way home on his trusty and rusty and squeaky police bicycle and the gates of the cricket club eventually closed after the winning home team celebrated their end of summer win.

Dondo lay down in his bed on the veranda he looked out onto the garden, he thought there is no better place than here in the cottage in Leafy Lane and this was his home and thankful he was to be living with a best friend Snowy and to be looked after by the Lady who was the best biscuit cook ever.

Dondo Turned to Snowball and said "it's been a good day Snowy, I hope you feel a little better now", Snowball was already fast asleep snoring peacefully next to his best friend,

Dondo the Magnificent.

Printed in Great Britain
by Amazon